小蟋蟀格里格里 Little Cricket Gery

丑娃娃和调皮鼠

The Ugly Doll and the Naughty Mouse

上海阿凡提卡通艺术有限公司　编绘

这本书属于＿＿＿＿＿＿

This book belongs to ＿＿＿＿＿＿

在一个幽静的角落里，

In a quiet corner,

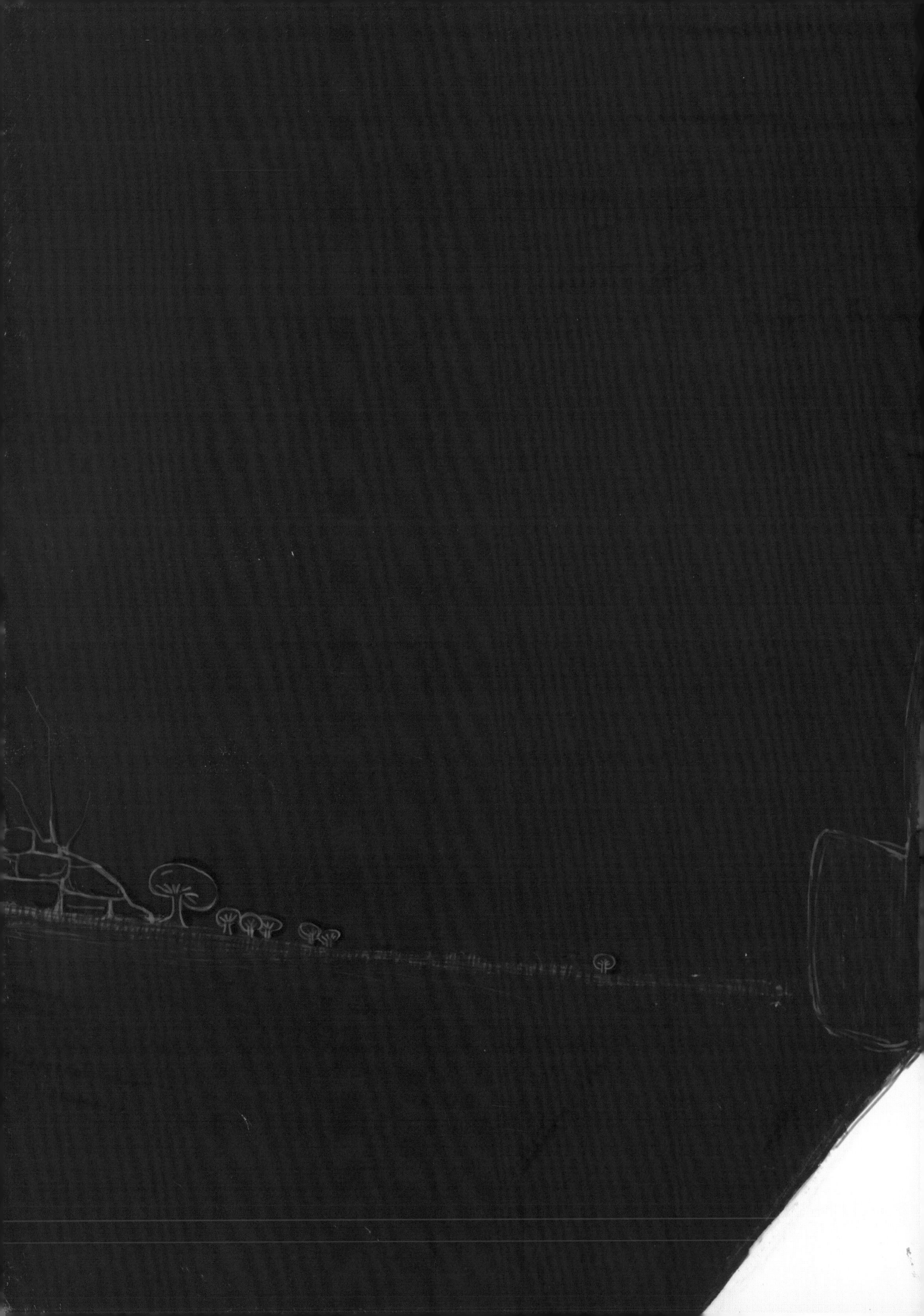

坐着一个丑娃娃，
在发呆。

sits an ugly doll, staring
into the empty air.

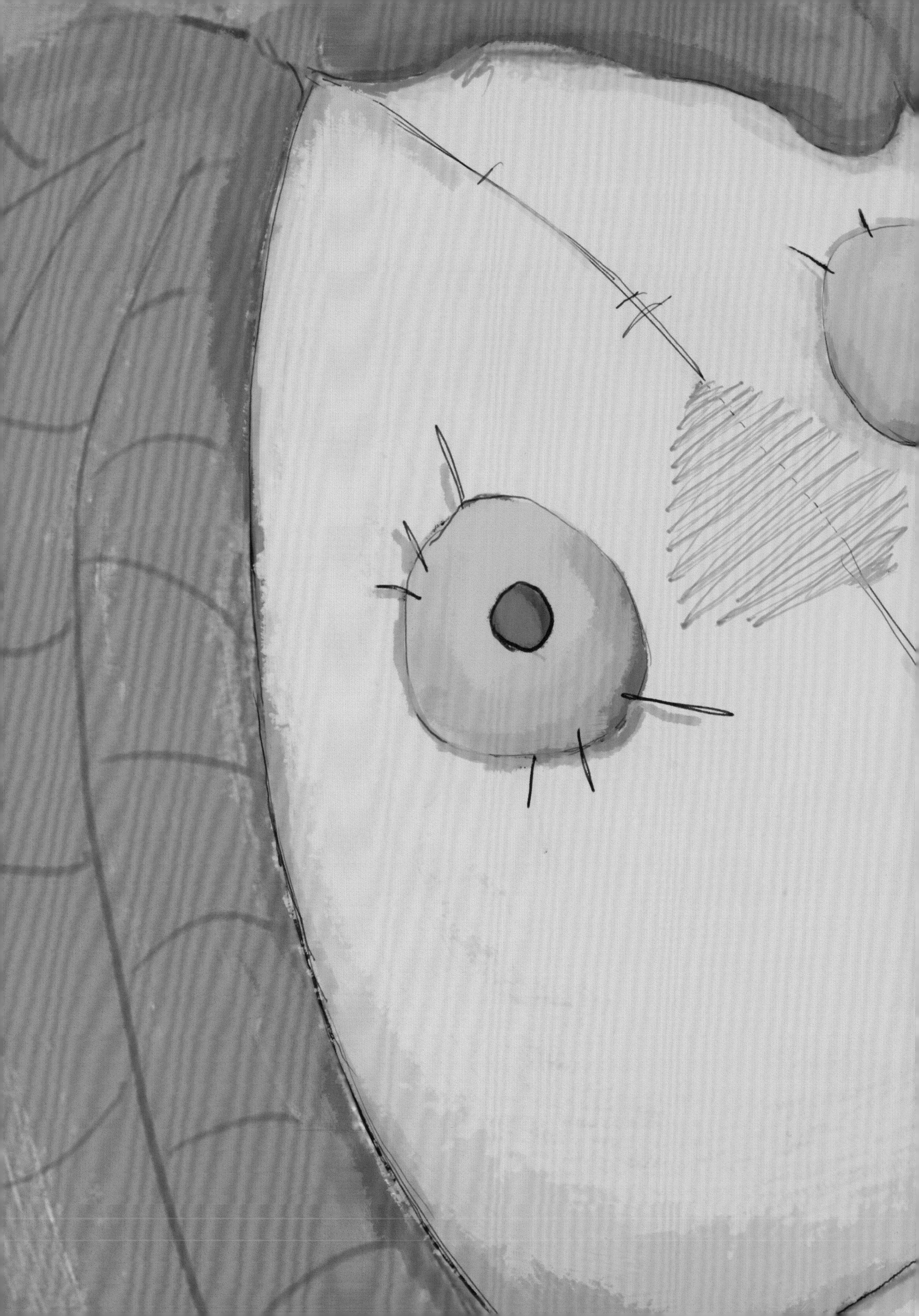

她为什么不快乐？
Why is she so sad?

原来她被主人丢弃了，
Because her owner has
胳膊也不见了……
abandoned her and she has lost both arms...

这是谁的胳膊？

Whose arms are these?

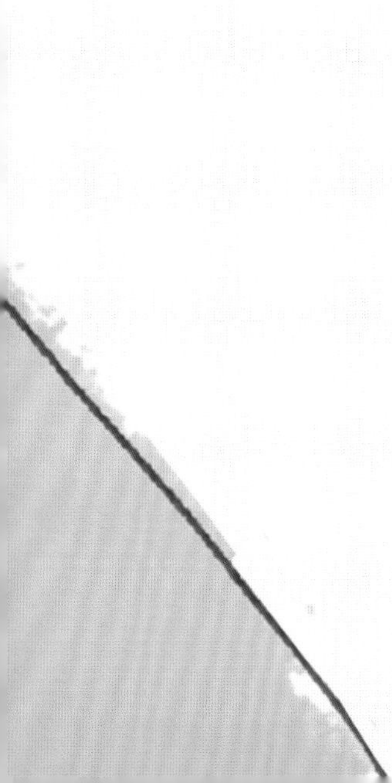

不远处来了一只调皮鼠，亲切地和她说话，像是她的老朋友一样。

From the distance comes a naughty mouse, talking closely with her, like an old friend.

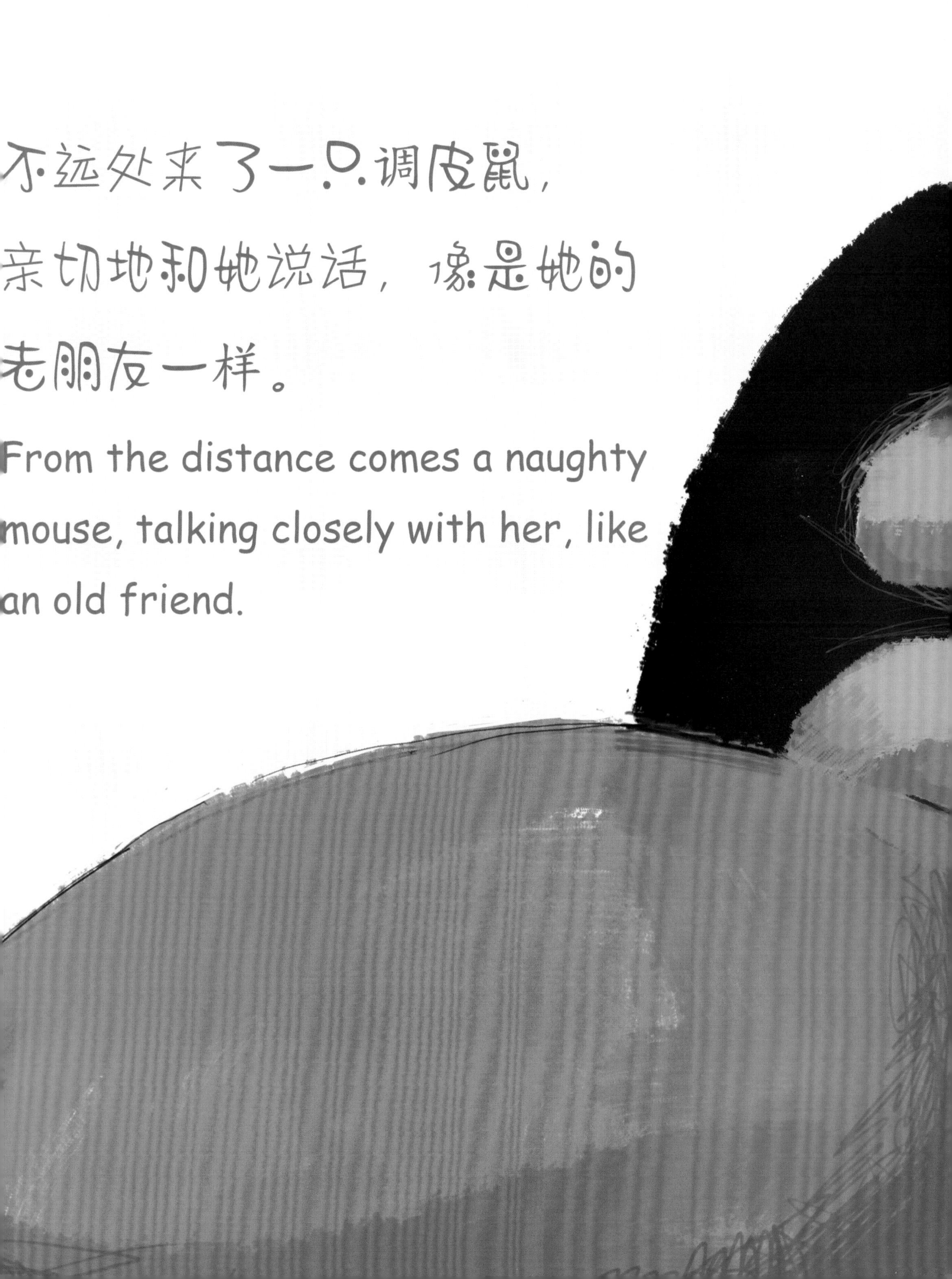

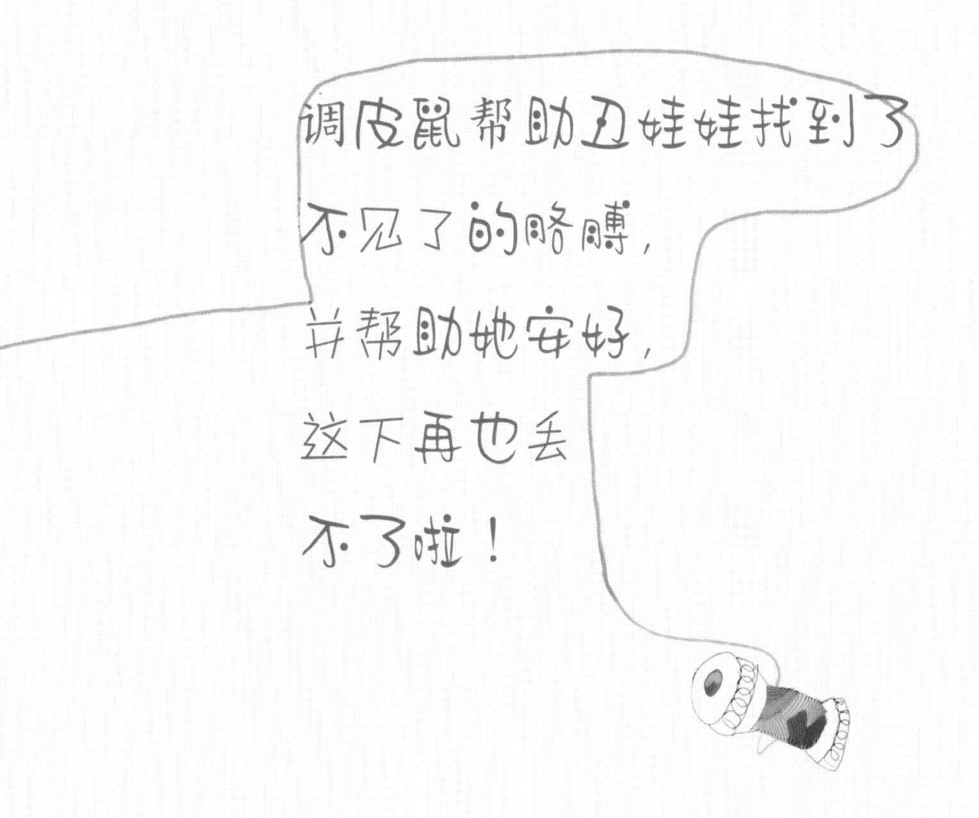

The naughty mouse finds the lost arms and fixes them onto her so tightly that they will never fall off again.

An unfamiliar world...
陌生的世界……

“可是，我的主人不见了，我也没有朋友……”丑娃娃说着，忍不住哭了起来。

“My master has gone and I have no friends...” The ugly doll says with tears in eyes.

不乖的小孩儿不是你的朋友。
The unkind child isn't your friend.
她把你丢弃了！
She has abandoned you and has cut her relationship with you...

不要伤心。我们一起玩儿。
Don't be sad. We
are all your friends!

雨伞爱你，从此你不必再害怕下雨。
The umbrella loves you and will shield you from rain.

小蜘蛛
爱你，
织个大太阳
给你温暖。

Little spider loves
you and will weave
a sun-like-net to warm you.

旧拎包爱你，
天天给你惊喜。
Old hand bag loves you and will
give you a surprise every day.

看我，变！
Look at me.
Transformed!

我们都爱你，
都希望你快乐，我们永远在一起！

We all love you. We all wish you happiness.
We will be together forever.

图书在版编目（CIP）数据

丑娃娃和调皮鼠/ 上海阿凡提卡通艺术有限公司编绘.
—北京：科学普及出版社，2014
（小蟋蟀格里格里）
ISBN 978-7-110-07795-5

Ⅰ. ①丑… Ⅱ. ①上… Ⅲ. ①儿童文学—图画故事—中国—当代
Ⅳ. ①I287.8

中国版本图书馆CIP数据核字(2013)第168953号

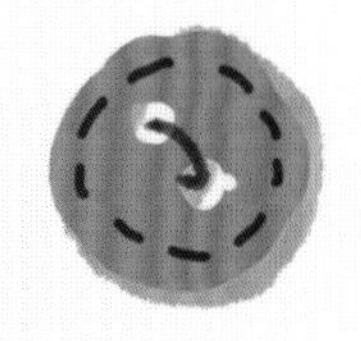

编　　绘　上海阿凡提卡通艺术有限公司
出 品 人　曲建方　郎　冰
监　　制　曲建方
美术设计　郎　冰
美术编辑　付旦妮
翻　　译　孙　艳
审　　译　[英]迈克尔·格雷厄姆
配　　音　张　佑　高西羽
出 版 人　苏　青
策划编辑　肖　叶
责任编辑　梁军霞　朱　颖
音频编辑　张　佑
封面设计　书袋熊
责任校对　林　华
责任印制　马宇晨
法律顾问　宋润君

科学普及出版社出版
北京市海淀区中关村南大街16号　邮政编码:100081
电话:010-62173865　传真:010-62179148
http://www.cspbooks.com.cn
科学普及出版社发行部发行
鸿博昊天科技有限公司印刷
*
开本:635毫米×965毫米　1/8　印张:4　字数:60千字
2014年1月第1版　2014年1月第1次印刷
ISBN 978-7-110-07795-5 / I·319
印数:1—10000册　定价:29.80元

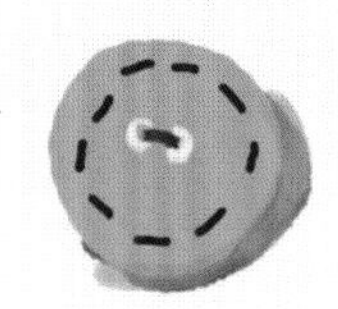

怎样开启你的TING笔

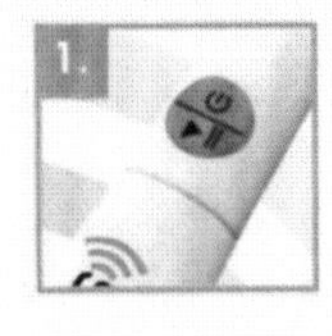

如需使用TING笔，请如图所示
长按开/关键2秒直至听到开机音乐。

用TING笔笔尖点击圆圈中心，你将听到一段音乐提示。这段音乐提示在你每次阅读点击TING书的时候都会出现。

现在你就可以使用TING笔并体验惊喜啦！

说明：如果你希望购买TING笔的配件、获得最新资讯或寻求帮助，请与我们联系或登录TING的门户网站：http://ting-pen.com